Dreams of Another Land

by

Peter Kenny

with a foreword by Colin Duriez

illustrations by Sue Bradley

Stichting
De Wereld Leest

ISBN: 978 94924 690 83

NUR: 306

Title: Dreams of Another Land
Author: Peter Kenny
Illustrated by: Sue Bradley
First Edition 2015 (published by Oloris Publishing LLC)
This edition: Second Edition 2018, second printing 2026
This version: The Standard edition
Copy editor: Sherry Larson-Rhodes
Proofreader: Margreet de Roo for Maneno Tekstredactie
Publisher: Stichting De Wereld Leest, Beverwijk (the Netherlands)

To all the inspirational people

I have met during my travels

near and far.

 Contents

The poems and tales in Peter Kenny's collection, he tells me, are inspired by his experience of J.R.R. Tolkien's world, but not in a literal way. Readers unfamiliar with Tolkien (there are still some) will find the collection evocative of other lands and distant places. Those knowledgeable of Tolkien might recognize some allusions to Middle-earth that are often concerned with atmosphere, and a feeling of familiarity that comes from a sense of place and their knowledge of stories of other worlds told by the master. Peter Kenny's poems and tales — or should I say Fortinbras Proudfoot's — concern elusive places and lingering stories that are best captured in words, but, like Tolkien's, are beautifully enhanced by illustrations, in this case by artist Sue Bradley.

What is Tolkien's world, that has so much inspired Peter Kenny, as no doubt Fortinbras Proudfoot's world will enchant his readers?

There is an unquenchable interest upon the part of readers (and film goers as well) in the landscapes that inspired authors like Wordsworth, the Brontes, Jane Austen, Thomas Hardy, D. H. Lawrence, Kenneth Graham, Lewis Carroll and many others. Tolkien was greatly inspired by the geography of England, and the West Midlands in particular, drawing upon actual places for names, images and even settings in his fiction, from the well-known *The Hobbit* and *The Lord of the Rings* to the less familiar *Farmer Giles of Ham* and *The Adventures of Tom Bombadil*. Even some English places that less directly may have influenced the shaping of the world of Middle-earth can have an extraordinary sense of familiarity for those who have read and loved his fiction. This may explain why places in England as far apart as Lydney Park in Gloucestershire to the Ribble Valley in Lancashire are claimed as inspiration. As well as the West Midlands, and counties like Berkshire and Oxfordshire, Tolkien also drew upon wider European geography and events, including a hair-raising visit to the Swiss Alps just before he started as a student at Oxford, and his experience of the apocalyptic vistas of the trenches of World War One. He saw the England and Britain he loved as rooted in the history, geography and languages of northwestern Europe. A primary model for Tolkien's work, the Early English poem *Beowulf*, takes place in is what is now Denmark and Sweden.

The very shape of Middle-earth intentionally alludes to the landmass of northern Europe, and its fictional history is set in an imagined ancient past of the West. Variants of Tolkien's invented Elvish have affinities with European languages (Finnish and Welsh). The Shire of the Hobbits is inspired by and deliberately evokes the rural world of Worcestershire and Warwickshire Tolkien knew as a child, much of it hidden today in the urban sprawl of Birmingham.

Peter Kenny's world picks up on the fact that Tolkien's Middle-earth has a sense of familiarity for readers and audiences that is far more widespread than only the inhabitants of Northwest Europe. He himself is from Australia, but is an inveterate traveller who has explored New Zealand and the European continent. Though we had met before, Peter on a visit to Britain typically travelled all the way to the far northernmost part of England to visit the English Lake District to see my wife and me — a region, like many in the world, that could have provided a visual setting for the stories of Middle-earth.

Like Tolkien's, Fortinbras Proudfoot's world seems centred at first in a world of rustic charm. This is a simple world, which nevertheless rejoices in tales, myths and legends from a larger world. In Tolkien, such a simple world is found most distinctly in the opening chapters of *The Lord of the Rings*. The larger world, in which dangers more clearly lurk and in which courage, faith and love more obviously are required, opens up as the story progresses, as it does even in its prequel, *The Hobbit*. A larger world is more the focus in Tolkien's *The Silmarillion*. In Proudfoot's poems and stories, the view is retrospective, placing a rustic world of little but courageous folk — the smallest of people — in the context of a larger world of danger, beauty and deepest longings.

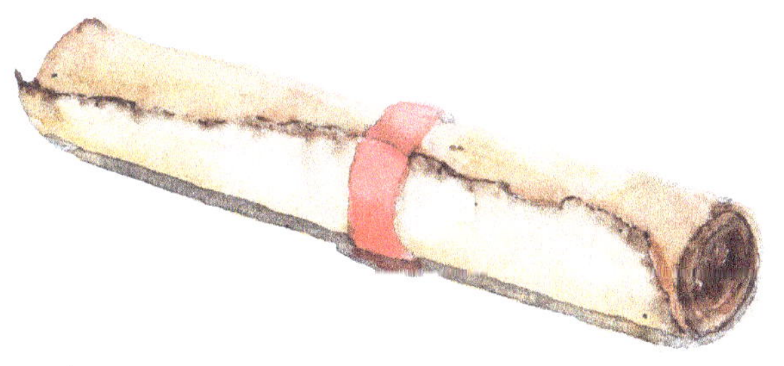

I recall that when I was young, I would sit with other children and listen to my uncle's stories, and at night I would lie in my warm bed and imagine myself adventuring to strange places with him. When sleep finally came to me I would dream of his adventures as though I was my uncle himself.

My uncle, Fortinbras Proudfoot, is a scholarly person. In his humble home he has many bookcases filled with books from all over. There are books in Elvish, and Dwarvish, books from far away lands and some from closer to home. There are books of poetry, and others of history, some on geography and some on cooking. There are many on the old tales of family heroes, and all their friends and their adventures! For they are his favourite tales of all.

In his youth he was a teacher, and many of the people in his village and the nearby towns knew Mr Proudfoot from their days at school. As such, wherever he went there was always someone keen to catch up, to share a meal and a chat with their wonderful friend Fortinbras.

He has, unlike many people of his village, travelled quite far from his home. He has been on journeys in his own land and has even travelled across the encircling seas to visit many places of legend and history.

My uncle is now very old but he still entertains us with many tales from his adventures of long ago to strange exotic lands. He has kept a journal of his adventures and within there are many stories in poetic verse form.

This book contains a collection of many of his writings. They include tales of heroic people, wizards, dragons, elves, and dwarves. There are also some tales of the smallest of people, who lived in a peaceful far away land of pastures, small villages, and green rolling hills.

I hope you enjoy reading these tales as much as I have enjoyed revisiting them once more to collate them for publication.

This collection of my uncle's work I have called

Dreams of Another Land

The Adventure Begins

Dreams of Another Land

Sitting by the open door
Dreaming of a place where adventure lies,
Staring at the far blue hills
Seeing the birds as they fly high.
They are flying to far away
To the hills and places far beyond,
The little boy sits and stares,
And he's dreaming of tales from another land.

Thinking of his uncle's tales
Telling of places and people so strange,
Looking in the old brown chest
Holding items that are so rare.
They are items from far away
From the lands and kingdoms far beyond.
The little boy sits and stares
And he thinks of legends from another land.

Packing up his little bag,
Placing in it all the items he needs;
Picking up his wooden sword,
He checks again his list of plans.
He is planning to go away
To the lands and kingdoms far beyond.
The little boy stands and stares
Then he steps on the road to another land.

SMALLEST OF PEOPLE

The land I love is in my senses:
The fragrance of flowers,
The sweet green grass,
The singing of birds,
The babbling of brooks.
It's where my true love lives,
It's where my heart lies.

The Smallest of People

In the North-West of our lands,
A small green country lies.
Home to the smallest of people,
Beneath the bluest skies.

Happy people they are,
Living a peaceful life,
Tending their gardens
And their fields alike.

They love riddles and games,
Pipe smoking and ale,
And plain simple food
Any time of the day.

Generous of heart
To all they invite,
They give away gifts
To toast a good life.

Distrustful of strangers,
They keep to their own.
In affairs of the world,
No interest is shown.

They're viewed by outsiders
As timid and slow,
Never seeking adventures
Just staying at home.

But…
They are the most soft-footed of people,
Both clever and shrewd,
And in a tight place,
Their courage is true.

And the day will come,
When they will be admired in awe,
For they will change,
The fortunes of all.

Adventure Under Southern Skies

They came from many lands,
They came to seek adventure;
Adventure under southern skies.
Together one night they made their plans,
Planning carefully all the days to come,
For their great adventure.

The road they travelled on
Led to a special township
Where all the houses had round doors.
The travellers enjoyed a day most pleasant
Taking with them memories to be shared,
Of this great adventure.

Travelling down the road,
They saw the great volcanoes,
Including the mountain called Doom.
They followed pathways in others' footsteps,
Seeking for locations that are famed,
In a great adventure.

Finally, the road it led
To the Premiere City,
And thousands were gathering there.
They gathered to celebrate an event.
A Celebration never to forget,
Of a great adventure.

It was the biggest event
In our recent memory
For the smallest of people.
People now we have come to admire,
The heroes in a story we love,
About a great adventure.

They came from many lands,
They came to seek adventure;
Adventure under southern skies.
Their great journey continued many days,
And memories were taken home to share,
Of their great adventure.

Mushrooms

Dark… Night!
Four halfling lads set out.
The air it made them shiver,
The moon was just a sliver.

Sneak… Quiet!
There was no one about.
They crept along the hedgerow,
Staying quiet and keeping low.

Hoo… Hoot!
A strange noise in the night.
An old owl in a tree top,
Had startled them to a stop.

Look… See!
Lights shining through the trees.
The farmer's house was alight,
But their goal was now in sight.

Go… Quick!
So little time to pick.
There were mushrooms all around.
The youngsters grabbed all they found.

Bark!… Bark!
The farm dogs were awake.
Four halfling lads took to flight,
Running quickly through the night.

Run!… Run!
This wasn't so much fun.
Racing frightened down the lane,
Safely home they hoped to gain.

Hip!… Hooray!
"We whistled all the way.
Found the mushrooms in the park,
And bravely walked in the dark.
Nothing frightened us at all!"
Well, that's the story they told to all.

seeds

The Gardener

He returned to the home that he loved
For so long he'd been away.
He had travelled far to foreign lands
No one thought that he'd return.

But returning to his cherished home
He found that now all had changed.
Now ruin scarred a country once fair
Many trees so loved had gone.

A gardener well known both far and wide
He vowed he would heal its scars.
He carried with him a precious gift
A small box of dust most fine.

He travelled for months throughout the land
Planting saplings where he went.
He added to each a grain of dust
And came Spring new trees grew forth.

He planted at last a silver nut
In a green field fond to all.
Soon grew there a tree of beauty rare
Covered with flowers of gold.

He remembers the time long ago
In a land of golden trees;
A gardener's gift the lady gave
He now used to save his land.

A SHORT TALE BY
FORTINBRAS PROUDFOOT

On the side of the hill, an elderly couple were sitting on a small bench under a small tree watching their grandchildren playing with cousins and friends on the Party Field in the shade of the great golden tree. Laughter and squeals of delight drifted up from the field below as the children chased one another and ran about on the soft green grass.

Planted years ago to replace the tree that was felled by thoughtless men, the golden tree has grown to great proportions and is renowned far and wide. It is said the tree is magical and brings good fortune to those who walk and sit beneath its branches. Over the years young lovers have declared their love under its silver boughs and many have been married in its shade.

As the elderly husband's thoughts went back to a time long ago, his wife placed her head on his shoulder. He thought of a distant time in a distant land where many such trees grew in a magical forest. The White Lady who lived in that forest gave him a small grey box decorated with one rune, a 'G'. Within the box lay a seed in special fine dust. Through many dangers he carried that box and brought it back to his beloved home. He planted the seed near the stump of the old tree and a beautiful tree with silver bark and golden blossoms quickly grew.

Legend tells of how when the tree bloomed in the following year all the surrounding countryside be-

came golden from the flowers that grew; and in that first spring when the tree blossomed, many children were born who were fairer than those of previous years. In subsequent years the children born seemed to have a new quality never before seen and many had golden hair.

As if she read his thoughts, his wife raised her head and looked into his eyes and whispered, "You brought magic and beauty home with you."

He looked into her eyes and saw starlight there and on her lips that youthful smile he had loved since he was very young.

He replied with a smile, "I came home to magic and beauty."

She closed her eyes and kissed him lovingly on his lips, a kiss as loving as their first kiss many years before.

Then she placed her head back on his shoulder and held his hand in hers.

They both smiled and felt young love again as they watched their grandchildren playing with cousins and friends on the Party Field in the shade of the great golden tree.

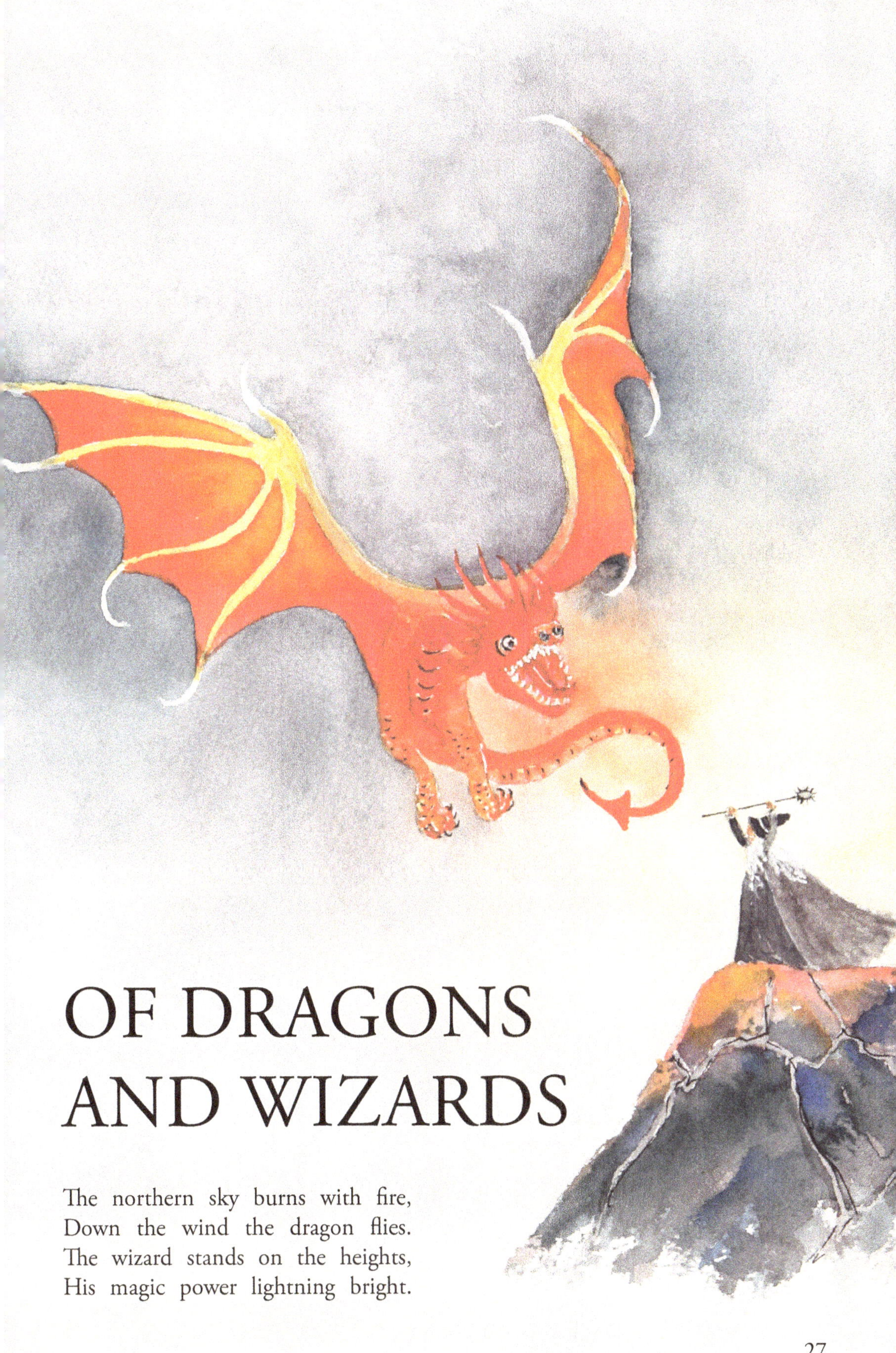

OF DRAGONS
AND WIZARDS

The northern sky burns with fire,
Down the wind the dragon flies.
The wizard stands on the heights,
His magic power lightning bright.

The Dragon Beneath the Golden Tree

We haven't seen a dragon round here for many an age,
Now found only on a storybook page.
My uncle doesn't know
About the one that we see
By the village garden
Beneath the golden tree.

At month's end he visits us
And tells us tales of ancient times.
Upon his back he carries us
And flies us high up into the sky.

With scales the brightest red,
With bat-like wings and big long tail.
He has white teeth that are gleaming,
And his large eyes they are beaming.

A magic dragon he is,
Seen only by the children's eyes.
For one full day he plays with us,
Then evening comes and away he flies.

We haven't seen a dragon round here since I was a child,
Now found only in places that are wild.
That, my uncle tells me,
But he doesn't know
About the dragon we see
Beneath the golden tree.

A magic dragon visits us beneath the golden tree,
Where children play with him happily,
A day will come,
When no more he'll return.
Or will the magic leave me?
Then him, I'll no longer see.

On Yuletide's Eve

On Yuletide's Eve, the shire is peaceful and quiet;
Children are tucked in bed for the night.
The Dragon arrives to visit his friend,
Someone he's known for such a long time.

In shire homes tonight
Children will sleep through the night.
In dreams they'll see him high,
A dragon flying
In the moon's silvery light.

On Yuletide's Eve, the shire is peaceful and quiet;
Children are tucked in bed for the night.
The Dragon arrives to visit his friend,
Someone he's known for such a long time.

Into the sky they fly,
Carrying gifts for all the shire.
By every door's light,
A delightful surprise
They'll leave for every child.

On Yuletide's Eve, magic is everywhere;
A dragon flies high through the air.
With morning's first light the children will rise,
And at their front doors presents they will find.

A Celebration Never to Forget

Exploding brightly up so high,
Wizard's magic lights up the night's dark sky;
There's gold and red, then green and blue,
Bursting flames of rainbow's every hue.

Fluttering dancing little lights
Wizard's magic for children brings delight
Little children they laugh and run
Chasing fairy lights made just for fun.

Fiery dragon roaring up high
Wizard's magic soaring through the dark sky
It swoops down low then up again
Bursting into brilliant rainbow rain.

The biggest party in our memory.
A night for people to be merry,
People came from all around
To celebrate a life renowned.

The tables were set with plenty of food
And the finest ale had been brewed
Music played throughout the night
Singing, dancing under bright lights.

Festive gathering to behold.
Families, children, and the old.
It was a celebration
A celebration never to forget.

The Wizard's Journeys

We are told of the wizard's journeys
Countless tales we have heard.
Years of numerous wanderings
To many places far and wide.

To the white city of men he rode,
To search for tales of old.
And there in those ancient stories
He found the legend he sought for.

It is known he rides a great white horse
Honoured by the horse lords.
The greatest horse owned by their king,
A gift from the golden hall.

Men whisper of his special friendship
With the white sorceress,
Whose kingdom lies in the forest
Where the trees have golden leaves.

It is said he's crossed the great river
To meet the woodland king,
Then travelled further to the east
To visit the mountain dwarves.

Friends say he meets a strange traveller
In the old crossroads inn.
He visits the hidden valley,
A place where elves live in peace.

And now I hear with great surprise,
The wizard has arrived
To entertain with fireworks,
All the children of our shire.

Three Stone Trolls

On a little-used path
In a forest remote,
Passers-by will behold
The strangest of sights.

In a tree-ringed space
Three large statues are found,
Of creatures most fearsome
Now forgotten in time.

Three stone trolls they are,
Once feared by travellers,
Now perches for birds
And playgrounds for critters.

A tale from the past,
Says a party of dwarves
Were caught by the trolls
When passing that way.

A wizard most grey,
He rescued those dwarves
And turned those nasty trolls
To cold, grey stone.

This story has changed
With the passing of time,
But they don't change,
Those three stone trolls.

The Blue Wizards

Two old wizards dressed in blue
Once this way passed through.
In records of old it is said
Upon our shores they did tread.
Also there came another three,
From across the western sea.
By the divine all were sent
To give the free encouragement.

Two old wizards dressed in blue
Strode as men young and true.
A dusty road along they tread,
Approaching mountains that are red.
None remember what they're called,
Peaks by which the East is walled.
Beyond laid lands of mystery
Not known in our histories.

Two old wizards dressed in blue
Vanished eastwards it is true,
About their mission it is written
The dark forces they did weaken.
One became the east helper,
The other, the darkness slayer.
Two old wizards dressed in blue
Came with wisdom from the west.

The Dragon's Hoard

In the Northern Mountains,
The Dwarves built mighty halls,
And in the caves deep below
Great treasures they did mine.
Their kingdom was renowned
Throughout the northern realms,
Their metal work and their gems
Were sought by one and all.

Their reputation spread,
But came to evil ears,
And a dragon soon set out
To seek their fabled halls.
He found the mighty doors
To the Dwarves' treasure halls.
There he slew the Dwarven King
And the King's youngest son.

The dragon took the halls,
He drove the Dwarves away.
He gathered the entire hoard
To make a precious bed.
The treasure he did count
And memorised the lot.
He slept and dreamt evil deeds,
Destruction, fire and death.

For many, many years,
People feared his lair.
No one came to challenge him
Or seek his golden hoard.
But as the decades passed,
The dragon he grew old;
In old age he slept too much
And let his guard be down.

One day whilst deep in sleep,
He dreamt a thief would come,
And enter his treasure hall
To take his hoard away.
Awakened from his dream,
A man before him stood.
Then a spear pierced his heart;
The dragon's fire went out.

The man took all the hoard
For his people and kin.
This brought them into conflict
With Dwarves who claimed it too.
The dispute it was settled,
The people southwards went,
Taking with them dragon gold,
A portion of the hoard.

Years turned to centuries.
The Legends grew and grew.
Stories of the dragon's hoard
Were told throughout the lands.
There is one tale written,
Of a lady much praised,
Who gave a small champion
A prized horn from that hoard.

AGES LONG AGO

On the mountain standing,
To the wind he's calling;
Eagles soaring over lofty heights.
Light of day is fading,
The host it is leaving;
Boat shining silver in the sky.

Queen of Earth

Tall tree under heaven
With golden crown on top
Branches spill a dew of golden drops.
Other shapes perceived
Tall woman often seen
She walks this world wearing shades of green.

Lover of all nature
Lover of the earth
Curing all that evil's marred and hurt.
Drives away the fears
Wipes away the tears
She's mother to all nature here on earth.

Forests green with towering trees
Pastures and the golden fields
Songs of power creating life devised
And in the new morning light
Plants and creatures come to life.
Bringing fruit to all the earth
Revered Queen of Earth.

Light from silver flower
Light from golden fruit
In the sky as sun and shining moon.
The darkness it is fading
The evil it will fall
The magic of a mother's gift to all.

Creator of the Dwarves

They called him the maker
Maker of the land
Making everything metal and stone.
Fashioning all substance
The mountains and the land
Creation of the lands home to all.

Of crafts he's the master
Master of great skill
Mastering crafts for finest things.
Craftsmanship he teaches
His students learn so well
Creating rarest jewels unsurpassed.

He's known as the creator
Creator of the dwarves
Creating fathers for seven clans.
Hardiest of races
With the gift of long life
Caverns of the earth they did mine.

His people are miners
Miners of the deep
Mining metals and precious stones.
Greatest of craftsmen
They craft beautiful things
Creating rarest jewels unsurpassed.

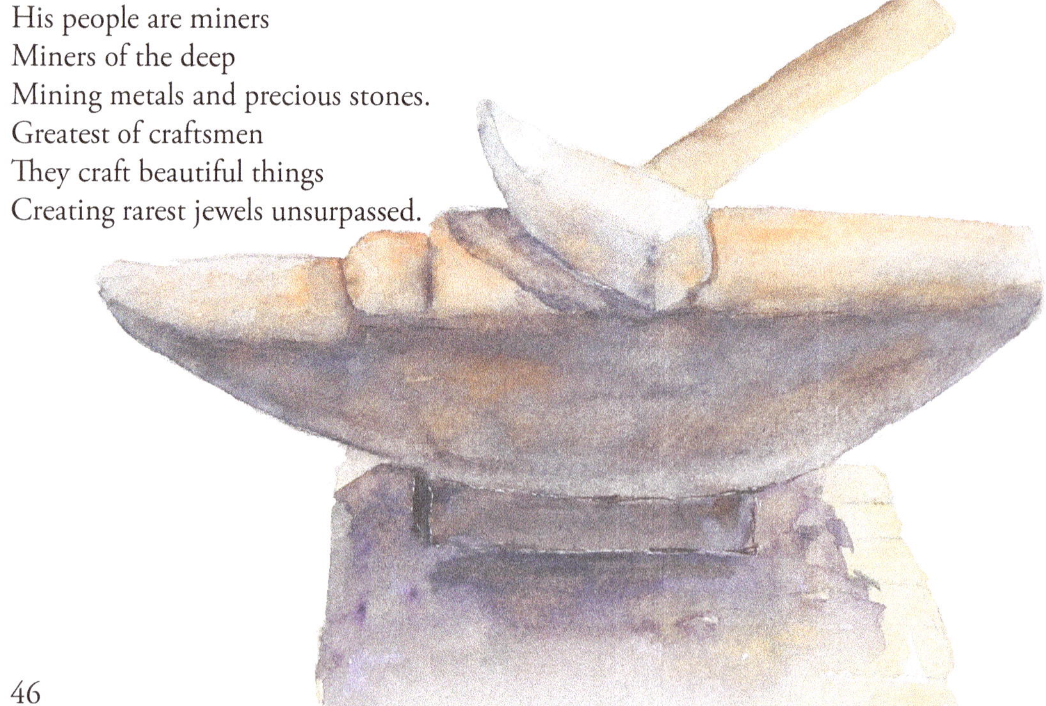

The Outlaws

So many men marched off to war,
But none were to return.
They fell in the north lands,
Wastelands full of grief;
Where the mighty lords did battle,
The fallen were heaped high.
With the tidings of great loss,
Many tears were shed.

Two mighty chieftains rode to war,
Two brothers of renown;
There from that far north land,
Neither would return.
Their sons too young remained at home,
But soon they had to hide;
As the darkness spread over lands,
Outlaws they became.

The legends tell us of their deeds,
In times of great despair;
They roamed through the dark lands,
Never did they meet.
One son was cursed by the darkness,
Even his greatest deed;
From his cousin new light grew,
Bringing peace to all.

Morning Star, Evening Star

In an age long, long ago,
Wandering through an Elven wood,
A lone warrior did espy
A maiden beautiful to behold.

As dark as the shadows was her hair,
And bright starlight shone in her eyes;
Golden flowers were on her cloak
And blue as the sky was her dress.
An Elven Princess was this maiden,
The "Morning Star" of her people.

Hopelessly in love he did fall,
This mortal man her heart did win.

But her father, the Elven Lord,
On their new found love he did frown.
To be betrothed to his daughter,
This mortal man seemed not worthy,
With his people scattered and few,
And his heritage dispossessed.

A high price was set by the Lord
To win his only daughter's love.
He set a task to undertake
That seemed difficult to achieve.
With faith, wisdom, and steadfast love,
The Princess gave her lover strength.

Against the Dark Lord,
He would succeed,
Against the darkness,
The tide would turn.

The Princess chose a mortal life,
To remain with the one she loved.
After enduring many trials,
In peace they lived for many years.

In this Age, not long ago,
Wandering through an Elven wood,
A lone warrior did espy,
A maiden beautiful to behold.

As dark as the shadows was her hair,
And Elven light shone in her eyes.
Silver and blue coloured her cloak
And gems like stars were on her brow.
An Elven Princess was this maiden,
The "Evening Star" of her people.

Hopelessly in love he did fall,
This mortal man her heart did win.

Lady of Hope

From a dying kingdom you escaped,
With family and the faithful.
New land, new life, new beginnings,
New home for all your people.

But The Shadow was never far behind
Pursuing all with great hate,
Bringing with it tragic war,
And the greatest grief for you.

In time The Shadow would be lifted,
The lord of darkness would be vanquished.
With joy and hope a New Age would dawn,
And all free people would rejoice.

In a fair land you dared to dream
Of a future full of hope.
The lines of grief etched on your face
With new joy would soon recede.

In your eyes new joy would be seen,
The proudest of mothers you'd become
Lovingly watching your youngest son
Talking and laughing with all his friends.

Soon he would accept his father's crown
And your son would ascend the throne.
With joy and hope a New Age would dawn,
And all free people would rejoice.

A new light would shine on the future,
New light shining for many years.
With your rare gifts of wisdom and foresight,
It was you who kindled that light.

Late in your years on the eve of war,
You conceived a fourth son to your lord.
And thus the ancient line would prevail,
Bringing new hope to the coming years.

With joy and hope a New Age now dawns,
And all free people now rejoice.
A new king now ascends the throne.
A new king descended from you,
From you, fair lady… Lady of Hope.

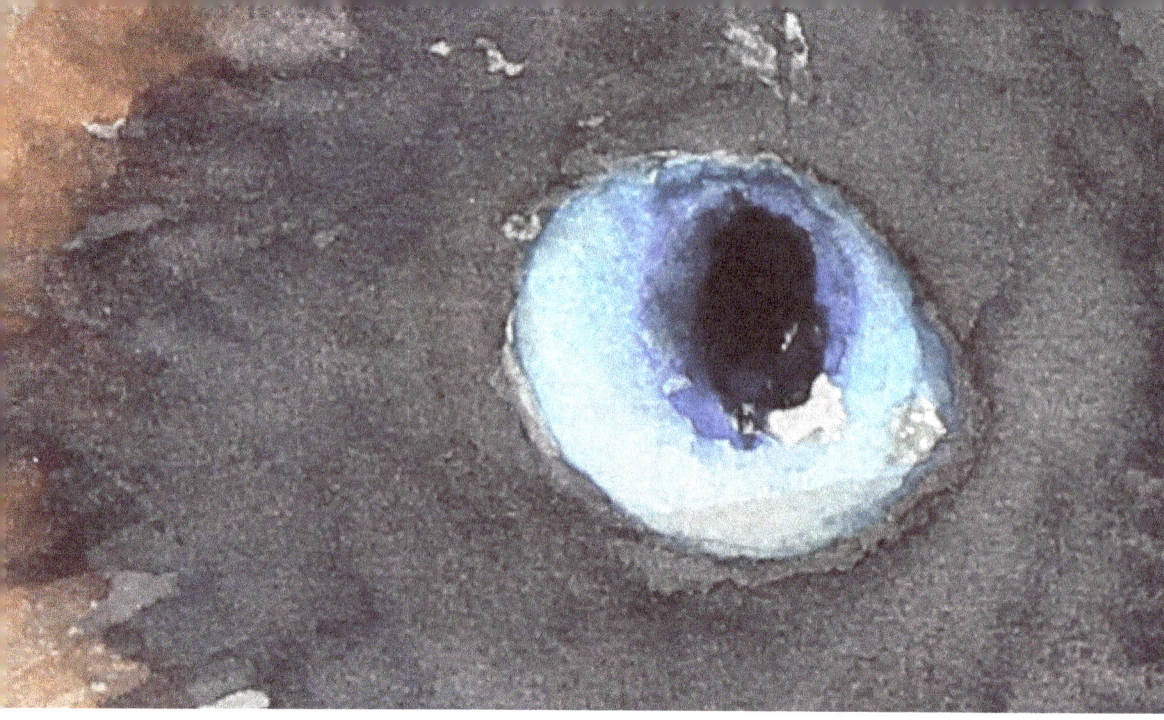

Queen of the Cats

Of the dark queen's cats,
A strange legend is told.
Her cats were cursed by all
In the ages of old.

Despising her husband
And his love of the sea,
Loveless and solitary
Her life soon came to be.

Shunning all beauty
And elaborate adornments
She chose black with silver,
To colour her garments.

She filled her garden
With sculptures tormented,
And trees and plants
Misshapen and twisted.

For her own wicked designs,
Sorcery she learned;
To the control of animals,
Her interest soon turned.

Legendary were her cats,
Nine black and one white.
They spied on the realm
Both by day and by night.

The darkest of secrets
Her cats did gather,
And the power she gained,
Brought fear to all others.

The outcries of his people
The King no longer ignored.
With force he removed her,
And exiled she was forever more.

The dark queen, alone with her cats
Was set adrift on the open sea;
Blown southwards to parts unknown
She sailed out of history.

What fortunes befell her,
It is nowhere told,
For her name was erased
From the records of old.

The Exile's Return

Exiled from his ancient home
The passing years had added pain.
Feeling the deep loss of his people
He found no peace for his hurt soul.
He yearned for a happier time
When peace was in his land.
He often dreamed of his home,
The kingdom where he was born.

Memories of his kingdom home
The greatest halls in all the north.
A time of freedom for his people,
They lived in peace for many years.
There they mined for all treasures
And made the finest things;
Greatest craftsmen of the north,
The ancestors of his home.

He lived in a foreign land
Where every day seemed just the same.
His ancient culture was deep in him
And voices called for him to leave.
He heard them calling to return
Back to the ancient halls;
To regain a kingdom lost
His own people's rightful home.

He remembers that peaceful night
When all the land seemed still and quiet;
Then from the north came fear and doom,
Death descending with dragon's fire.
The memories of that endless night
Bring visions that torment;
Desolation burns his heart
The tragic loss of his home.

Standing on a windswept hill
He's hearing calls that bring a sign.
This land's been burnt for years untold
But feelings tell him change is near.
From the long lake a message came
Bringing hope for the land;
Into the lake the dragon fell
Now freedom dawns for his home.

Seeing now in his mind's eye
A new kingdom of wealth so great.
The urge is deep to see the gold
Now waiting there for his return.
He always hoped this day would come
During the hopeless years;
At last he can reclaim his home
That ancient place where he was born.

AGE OF HOPE

The King and the Divine,
Their lives were entwined.
The seed they planted then,
Would now be born again.

The Captain From the North

In the years before there was a king,
From the north he did come,
A born leader of men,
A captain of great worth.

His emblem was a star and eagle,
His tunic gold-trimmed night.
He wore mail on leather,
A great sword at his side.

To the city of towers he came,
Riding a great dark horse,
Given by the Horse Lords,
For service to their king.

He was keen of eye and swift of foot,
A master of the sword,
A warrior so brave,
That men served under him.

Admired by the city's ruler,
His advice soon was sought,
On matters of defence,
The kingdom to protect.

The kingdom was forever threatened,
By raiders from the south.
Their fleet besieged the towns,
All up and down the coast.

Raising a small fleet of volunteers,
To the south they did sail.
On a dark moonless night,
The raiders' fleet was destroyed.

To honour him the city waited,
Return, he never did.
Bidding his men farewell,
To the east he did ride.

To where he rode is not known
Nor what his errand was.
The folk of the city
Continue to believe,
That soon a day will come,
When their captain will return.

Phantom of the Night

He rides like a phantom through the night,
From where he rides none can say.
With stealth he moves keeping out of sight,
And never seen by light of day.

Travellers say they have seen this stranger
Riding in the night.
Some say he keeps roads free of danger,
Both by day and by night.

On darkest nights he comes to the inn,
When he arrives none can say.
He sits for hours in conversation,
With an old man who's dressed in grey.

Mysterious is this tall dark stranger,
Who rides in the night.
Keeping us free from nearby danger,
Both by day and by night.

Some stories say he's an elven friend,
But who elves are none can say.
Perhaps a long-lived man of legend,
One from an age of yesterday.

There is little we know of this stranger,
Phantom of the night.
Our lives some say he keeps from danger,
Both by day and by night.

With Dawn Came Doom

Bringing to an end the long cold night
Sunrise spread across the valley quiet.
Songs of welcome birds began to sing
To new day's warmth the sun did bring.

Brightening sky shining in the east,
Western sky now signalled night's retreat.
Northern mists in morning's light departed,
But the sky to the south it darkened.

In a clear blue sky a black contrast,
Tidings that fortunes were changing fast.
Blackest clouds of war rose high in the sky
Approaching end of time now seemed nigh.

Quietness then descended all around,
In the valley there was now not a sound.
From the north a gentle breeze began,
An unexpected change was at hand.

All valley land began to tremble,
Then through the air a distant rumble.
Horns were sounding in the north,
The mighty horse lords now rode forth.

Into the valley the horse lords rode hard,
Headed by the golden king's vanguard.
Royal guardsmen and mighty knights,
All shining in the morning light.

A mighty host through the valley streamed
Beneath banners white horse on green.
Uncounted numbers all morning rode by
Towards the southern darkening sky.

The flowing host eventually it did cease,
The entire valley then returned to peace;
But coming doom in the air did impend
That the host rode to the world's end.

She sits by the window
And creates with love
A new banner of black
With stars made of gems

And there in the centre
A tree coloured white
Beneath a crown shining
Of silver and gold.

A banner for the new hope
She perceives in him
A banner for valour
A banner for kings.

Each day now she waits
For the end of shadow and war
The dawn of the light and the peace
When her lover she will meet once more.

He went to the shadows
A long time ago
A cold winter's evening
The company left too.

She dreams of a future
When all is at peace
And once more with him walking
Through flowers of gold.

She has chosen her future
Her destiny sealed
For the love of this man
She knows what it means.

Each day now she waits
For the end of shadow and war
The dawn of the light and the peace
When her lover she will meet once more.

They Stand There as One

To the north they gaze
At the black clouds climbing high.
They can see the lightning
Spreading across the sky.
All things become calm then,
Time seems to stand still.
They are waiting for a sign,
That this could now be the end.

On the wall they stand
In a north wind blowing strong;
Through their hair it's blowing
The raven and the gold.
Clasping hands together
They feel their hopes rise,
As the wind then tears the clouds,
And blows them all far away.

Then the sun shone through
And the black clouds disappeared.
They now see the river
Shining there silver bright.
All is calm everywhere,
Time again stands still.
They are waiting for a sign,
That the shadow now has passed.

Now as one they stand
In the sunlight shining strong.
It glows on them warmly
And covers them in light.
He kisses her softly,
They feel their love grow.
And the land now is shining
In the new age that is born.

A New Age of Freedom

A new age of freedom has now dawned in all the lands
Dark days now are just a memory
Peace has returned to people once enslaved
And a king of wisdom rules the land again.

Through shadows and certain death,
With faithful riding close behind,
Along forbidden paths he rode,
To seek assistance from forgotten men.

In the darkest hour he came,
With love-made banner flying proud.
His enemies before him fled,
He rode to triumph and great victory.

With the gift of healing hands,
He brought new hope to wounded souls.
Through his courage and humble heart,
Respect and trust he won from everyone.

On a day in springtime to our land did ride the king,
Accompanied by his lovely queen.
They brought with them a future of hope,
The king and his queen bless our land again.

A new age of freedom has now dawned in our own land
Dark days now are just a memory
Peace has returned with a future of hope
An age of freedom dawns in all the lands.

Warrior Princess

Pennants flapping black and red,
Riders wearing silver mail,
A dragon was their crest.

They came riding from the east,
With them bringing rarest gifts
And message of new peace.

In morning's light those riders came
And in its light we saw her
Riding there for all to see,
Dressed all in black a warrior.

War sword hanging at her side,
Knives for fighting on her back,
This maiden walked with pride.
With all bowing to the king,
Alone standing she stood there,
As equal to the king.

In evening's light she came in white,
And in moon's light we saw her,
Shining there for all to see,
A princess now most beautiful.

In morning's light her horse she rides
And at first light we see her,
The princess and the warrior,
And future hope that rides with her.

Old Friends

It was late morning and the sun had climbed high into a clear blue sky. On a stone seat near the edge of the battlements a small grey-haired person sat gazing out towards the eastern horizon.

From this high position, the small person could see all the fields spread out between the city and the river like a patchwork of green, yellow and brown. On the fields various buildings small and large were randomly placed and some fields were dotted by different types of farm livestock.

Tracks and small roads criss-crossed the countryside which was divided into segments by three main highways, from the north, east and south. Along these highways he could see wagons, carts and horse riders travelling on some errand to and from the city's great gate.

While watching the traffic moving along the roads, his mind drifted back to a dark day sixty years ago when the same fields were criss-crossed by fiery trenches and clusters of dark tents erected on the fields. He remembered the thousands of troops moving in masses towards the city walls, all driven by one purpose, to destroy this city and the kingdom of the west.

Beyond the fields he could see the great river as its waters sparkled in the sunlight. On the far side of the river were low hills covered with lush green trees. Above these fair hills towered a steep wall of mountains, the peaks of which were like jagged teeth. Those peaks were tipped now by snow, a sign that winter had started but in this southern land winter was never too severe.

How all now looked different to his memories of long ago, when this land was covered in darkened gloom and those distant mountains were black and foreboding. Gazing eastwards he recalled how the darkness and doom had been driven away and soon after a new king was crowned. He was now an honoured guest of that same king and his lovely queen.

Just then he became aware of a tall man standing by his side. The man was dressed in the black and silver uniform of the citadel guards. Although tall and strong of stature, the man was quite old as his silver hair, grey beard and creased face revealed. The man smiled and said, "Friend, I heard of

your arrival and now I have finally found you."

The small person looked up at his visitor and immediately recognised him. They had met on a few occasions during the intervening years since their first encounter. He recalled that when they first met, this man had only been a young lad with whom he had spent an afternoon in this city, but that time was different; then on the eve of war, now was an age of peace.

Just then they heard horns blowing in the east. Looking in that direction, far off they could see a long column of riders and wagons emerging from the old city on the river.

Trumpets on the city walls were blown in welcome.

"Who are they?" the small person asked.

"Emissaries from a far eastern kingdom," replied the man. "Come, you will see. Let us go to the great gate below and welcome the king's visitors."

INTO THE WEST

Walking by the ocean at day's first light,
The sunlight glimmers on the sea;
And in the morning's light I see,
White sails spread to catch the breeze.
Here on this distant shore at day's first light,
I hear the white birds call to me;
And in those calls I clearly hear,
Voices from across the sea.

Final Farewells

The morning mist still drifted above the distant river, dew drops glistened on the leaves of bushes and white smoke rose upwards from one of the many chimneys of the great hall.

Near the great hall's main entrance a small greyhaired person sat in a chair holding a small horn which was decorated with silver and engraved with numerous horsemen.

As he sat there looking at the horn, he ran his fingers over the engravings of the tiny horsemen and his thoughts drifted back to a time over sixty years ago in a land far to the south. Closing his eyes, his mind saw the images and heard the sounds of a great farewell feast in a golden hall. There in that hall were gathered the greatest people and heroes, many of whom were dearest friends.

After the feast and as people said their final farewells before travelling back to their homes, the king's sister, a lady of great renown amongst the people of her land, gifted this exquisite horn to him for his bravery and services to her kingdom.

New images came into his mind from all those years ago, of one particular morning. He saw mist drifting above a far river and thousands of horsemen's helms glistening in the morning light as smoke rose upwards from the battlefield before him. Horns sounded and the earth trembled with the sound of horses' hooves as they charged to battle.

He rode with the lady to battle on that fateful day, the same lady who gave him this beautiful horn. They rode onto the field before the white city and there he aided the lady to vanquish a great evil from the land forever.

On that day and the days that followed, the free peoples won great victories over the armies of the dark lord, and with their victories a new age of peace and freedom dawned.

He opened his eyes and looked at the horn one more time and then he raised his eyes to gaze at the road that led from the river to the great hall where he waited.

He was awaiting the arrival of his dearest friend who had shared his adventures all those years ago. Now, together, they would go on one final adventure and visit old friends in those lands far away.

He had been master of this great hall for many years, and now he would gift the horn to his son who would become the new master.

Then, as he gazed down the road, in the distance, he saw, riding slowly out of the mist, his lifelong friend. The time had now come for final farewells.

He arose from his chair and walked slowly back into the great hall where his family and dearest friends were waiting. There they had prepared a farewell breakfast for his friend and him, before they departed on their final adventure.

Sail Away With Me

Sail away with me to the West;
Sail away with me
To a land beyond the sun.

Sail away with me to the West;
Sail away to where
The folk are fair to behold.

In my dreams
I see your golden hair,
Your eyes oh so blue,
And the beauty of your smile.

I want to walk with you
On far white shores
And lie on soft green grass.

I want to walk with you
Beneath blue skies
And dream of days to come.

There we can sit on a high hill top
To watch the sun rise
And feel its warmth together.

Hoping soon that you will come
And sail with me on my ship.
Sail away with me to the West;
Sail away with me.

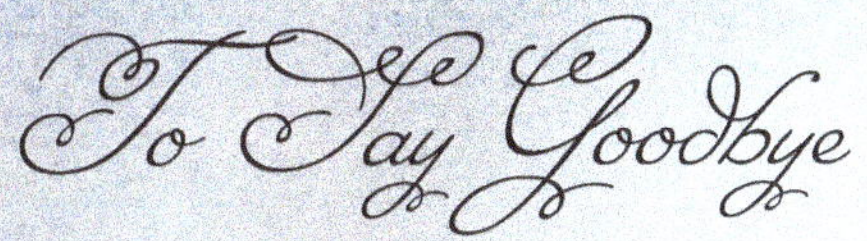

To Say Goodbye

For oh so long now
You've lost the life you knew
You're living on in pain
Hoping for a day
When joy will come again
But your hopes grow and fade
As the days pass you by
Is it time to say goodbye?

Your closest friends know
The horrors that you've seen
But do they understand
The deepest of your hurts?
Even time cannot heal
The feelings deep inside
Is this where you belong
Or do you say goodbye?

One morn when all is still
You know that they will come
To carry you away
And ease the pain you feel.
Will loved ones understand
The reason you depart
To start a better life
And why you say goodbye?

On a day when all is calm
A ship will come to port
To carry you away
And sail into the west.
And memories will fade
Of things that caused the pain
To the life you leave behind
You can now say goodbye.

An Elven Lady So Fair

Across the wide encircling seas
There lies a distant land,
Where mountains touch the sky
And clouds caress them high.

The forests on the mountain slopes
Are full of nature's gifts,
And crystal waters flow
In the valleys far below.

And in those green vales
Between the mountains,
They say the fairest people live.

She appeared at first in a dream
From that far distant land,
Her hair is golden sheen
Her eyes the softest green.

Out of the west the swan ships came
Arriving on our shores;
On a bright starry night,
A fleet all glistening white.

And when she sailed here
In her white swan ship,
She brought the rarest gifts to give.

Her smile brings sunshine to the world,
Her laughter brings such joy;
She makes all people glow
Wherever she does go.

Her heart is kind and full of warmth,
She shows the gentlest care.
The time that she was here,
A memory oh so dear.

And then she left
And went into the west,
To return and live
With the elves so fair.

The Ancient Shipwright

Yearning for undying lands
In every ship they sail for home,
The land they leave now holds no joy for them
With memories of those who've died.
They quietly board the waiting ships
To sail the open sea,
Always towards the setting sun
They sail into the west.

Being lord of the havens
In every age he's built their ships,
To cross the sea like those who've gone before
To sail along the one straight road.
Thus stands the ancient shipwright
Watching ships set sail,
He wonders if a day will come
When he will sail to the west.

He waits for that final day
When tidings tell the time has come,
That those who wear the rings have now set out
And are riding down towards the sea.
When their white ship sails from sight
He'll know his task is done,
And on the final ship he'll sail
Far away into the west.

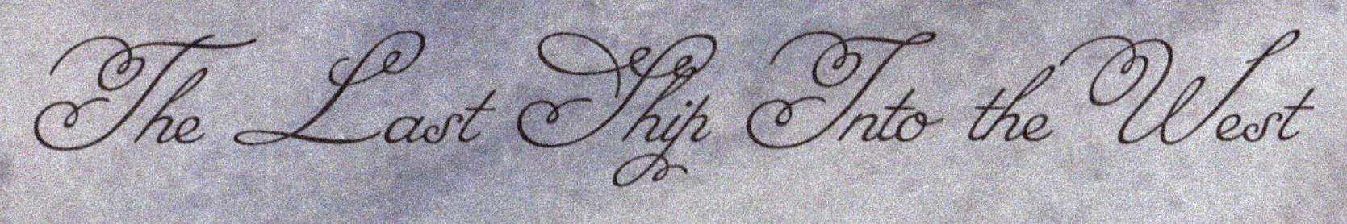

The Last Ship Into the West

On the headland she stood gazing out
Towards the western sea.
Her dress was gleaming white,
Her hair as dark as the night.
No recognition did she show
As I came by her side;
Her gaze had shifted now
To the harbour far below.

A great white ship was setting sail
To the far western shores.
She knew just what this meant,
This last ship into the west.
The ship it sailed, towards the sun
Sailing along a golden stream.

Together we watched that final ship
Sailing across the sea;
Then into the golden light
It sailed slowly from our sight.
Suddenly she raised both her arms
As the sky turned to gold,
A great wind then did blow
From the fading western glow.

Her raven hair streamed out behind,
Her dress was tinged with gold,
Then the wind it raised her sleeves
Like wings gliding on a breeze.
And in that moment it appeared
That she would simply fly away.

Finally she lowered both her arms,
The sun sank into the sea
The wind slowly died away,
Calm greeted the end of day.
With strands of hair covering her face
Towards me she then turned.

As she brushed hair aside
Elven light shone in her eyes.

A crystal tear on her cheek,
Sparkled in the day's last light.
I wiped it with my fingertips,
A smile appeared on her lips.
Gently she took my hand in hers
And then she kissed me on my cheek.

As we turned our backs to the sea,
I clasped her hand in mine;
And in the fading light of day,
A fair green land before us lay.
Distant houses were lighting up,
As the day turned to night.
Arm in arm we walked down the road,
Towards the place we now called home.

A place where we could dream together
Of a future now, full of peace and hope.

The Adventure Will Continue

Afterword

Dreams of Another Land had its beginnings in the classroom where I often read *The Hobbit* to my students and developed literacy units based on *The Hobbit* and *The Lord of the Rings*. Through these units I encouraged pupils to write stories and poems about imagined lands, characters and creatures inspired by Tolkien's stories. I often wrote poems and short stories as examples for students to inspire them. Some of those poems have been included in this publication.

When I retired, I continued writing as a hobby and I have often used some of my stories, songs and poems in presentations for children and adults at various venues both at home and overseas.

Many of the poems in this publication were inspired by people I have met at home and during my travels through Europe and to New Zealand. Others were written in response to places, events and experiences during those travels.

"Morning Star, Evening Star" was originally a classroom composition, which I re-wrote and expanded for my visit to Tolkien's gravesite in Oxford, where I read it in the company of other devotees.

"Adventure Under Southern Skies" was inspired by my journey to the world premiere of the first *Hobbit* movie in Wellington.

"Warrior Princess" is a poem about a young friend in Brisbane who loves to cosplay at conventions, dresses at our events as Arwen, and is also a horse lover who loves riding her own horse.

Lovers of Tolkien's Middle-earth will recognise many of the characters and stories referred to in these written works but often with subtle differences. Those who are not devotees to Tolkien's stories will hopefully find the imagery in each poem and story a world of fantastic imagination.

My alter ego, Fortinbras Proudfoot, was created a decade ago when I was doing *The Hobbit* as a unit of work with my Year (Grade) Seven class. All the children were given Hobbit names which were created by an online word generator. The teacher had to have a Hobbit name, so I modified mine into one I liked, which was Fortinbras Proudfoot. I have kept the name ever since and use it as my pen name for poems and stories I write, and of course it was selected for my Children's Literacy Foundation.

Acknowledgements

This book, the second edition of *Dreams of Another Land*, came to fruition through the kind offer of Jeroen Bakker of Stichting De Wereld Leest in The Netherlands to take on the publishing requirements for my upcoming publications in the future. To Jeroen I am most grateful for opening up a new door for my future writings.

For a number of years I have dreamt of having my stories or poems published as a book for people to enjoy. This is my first venture into the world of published written work and I am indebted to a number of people for bringing my dream to fruition. This book is mainly an anthology of poems. Most of the poems within these pages have been inspired by friends at home, people I have met during my overseas travels and events I have attended.

My first acknowledgement goes to Sue Bradley, whose wonderful artwork enhances these poems. Sue has become a co-partner in this publication and has also been a pleasure to work with. Co-operation and sharing of ideas has been an enjoyable experience as we slowly watched the project grow and develop into its final manuscript.

I am most grateful to Colin Duriez, well respected author, conference presenter and friend, who has always shown an interest in my projects and who has written a generous foreword for this my first publication.

A special thank you goes to Sherry Rhodes, who showed an early interest in my work and became my valued copy editor. Her suggestions at times led to part or whole rewrites of my work.

Members of the Local Brisbane Tolkien Fellowship have been encouraging towards my work and special mentions go to friends Trevor, Greg, and Phillip whose talent and displays of passion in costume making and role playing create wonderful subjects for writing. To Amy Bechly, whose enthusiastic response to my poetry writing sparked a period of prolific creativity and to Kirsten Burke whose Proudfoot essay, on which the opening story is based, helped a procrastinating writer break down the barrier of writer's block. The marvels of modern technology have also been a wonderful assistance to the project, bringing together the talents of people from The Netherlands, United States, England and Australia.

My former publisher, Oloris Publishing, unfortunately had to close but to Robyn Stone, and Lara Sookoo I am deeply indebted with gratitude for supporting my dream and bringing my first book to publication.

Most of the poems within these pages have been inspired by friends at home, people I have met during my overseas travels and events I have attended. Writing the poems in this book grew out of my passion for Middle-earth.

About: Sue Bradley, illustrator

Sue Bradley is an artist and illustrator based in the United Kingdom. Growing up with a strong interest in art and literature, she developed a passion for the works of J.R.R. Tolkien and other fantasy writers such as C.S. Lewis.

As a teenager, Sue was inspired by many artists of the fantasy genre, including Arthur Rackham, Roger Dean, George Underwood and Barry Godber. This led to many doodles on her school books of fairies, goblins, elves and other imagined creatures. In more recent times, Sue has been influenced by the illustrations of Alan Lee, John Howe, Brian Froud and Ted Nasmith.

Sue trained and worked as a biochemist before qualifying as a primary school teacher. However, throughout these years she continued to draw and paint, attend art courses and develop her artistic style. She now teaches painting to adults, art clubs and societies. Sue is represented by a gallery in Beckenham, Kent, U.K.

Website: www.suebradleyart.co.uk

About: Peter Kenny, author

Peter Kenny is a retired teacher based in Brisbane who possesses one of the most significant personal collections of Tolkien memorabilia in Australia and the world. Peter has had a passion for everything Tolkien for four decades and he has become a recognized authority in the field, sharing his knowledge and passion for Tolkien's stories with adults and children around the world through a series of presentations and events at schools, libraries, conventions and festivals.

During his forty years as a teacher he often used *The Hobbit* as a literacy unit in the classroom and shared Tolkien's world with hundreds of students through reading stories, composing and art.

Now retired, Peter writes poems, songs and fantasy stories inspired by Tolkien's Middle-earth as a hobby and shares his work in his presentations and with his friends.

His continuing passion and writing has led to a selection of his work being chosen for this publication.

MEMORIES OF ANOTHER LAND

Now available

ISBN 978 9492 4690 90

Further writings from the manuscripts of

Fortinbras Proudfoot,

which take us to that land familiar to us all.

The Beautiful Queen of Stars

Bright stars gleaming in the night,
Diamonds in the sky,
Gifts from the lady ever white;
Radiating with light,
Too beautiful for words,
She is queen of the stars shining bright.

We call on her in dark times,
Moments of despair,
Praying to her for brighter times;
Prayers she hears sent by us,
Our songs raised in praise,
She listens to our voices with love.

Night-time skies filled with gleaming stars,
Blossoms in a field of dark,
Dewdrop diamonds from a silver tree.
Down here on earth in starry light,
We now see in that sparkling sky,
Visions of her shining face,
The Beautiful Queen of Stars.

Lady dressed in shining white,
Radiant snow white,
Queen revered by one and all.
We rejoice in the light,
Of her gleaming stars,
She is queen of the stars shining bright.

The Clans Will Gather

Driven from their ancient homes,
Many they loved were left behind.
Scattered people across the lands to roam,
Their mourning would last a long time.
Some wandered to lands far away
Over mountain and plain,
Others resolved to find a way
To start life over again.

Gone are the old traditions,
None tell the fireside stories,
No merry tunes played by musicians,
No singing of ancient glories.
Hearts now are full of lasting pain,
Awful has been the cost.
Now only memories remain,
Of those loved ones they have lost.

In strong hearts a fire still burns,
Fire that will never be doused.
The wait is long as each season turns,
But spirits once more will be roused.
A day will come when friends shall meet,
And calls will cross the land.
Clans once more old oaths will repeat,
And their vengeance will be planned.

They will be drawn by the call,
To come and stand with their king;
From village, town and mountain hall,
Many will join the gathering.
And when all clans have joined at last,
They will march to the vale.
Evil had won there in the past,
This time their strength would prevail.

Now My Love, I Say Farewell

Once-fair lands around me
Are full of death and sadness.
With the darkness spreading
My vision has been dimmed,
And spring's music is now erased
By the beating drums of war.

Our world is slowly dying
As chaos spreads its dark tendrils,
And I know I may not survive
To see a new day dawn.
But despite this impending doom,
I feel your presence close to me.

Standing here alone
My thoughts drift to you, my love.
I see your smiling face,
I feel your tender touch,
I recall our first loving kiss
On a clear starry night.

Memories of younger days
When the world was peaceful and fair;
Of the spring days spent together,
As love grew in our hearts.
But with my heart now full of grief
Your smiling face fades from my view.

News that I now hear
Is oh so bitter, my love.
You stood in defiance
When sudden flame approached.
Protecting home and family
You fell to your final doom.

I must face my future choice
And overcome my grieving heart.
To see your beauty one more time
I am full of yearning.
But now our love is lost to me,
I wonder how I will survive.

As darkness envelops the sky
And the flames of war fast approach,
I turn my back to lands I loved
And memories oh so dear.
With all my kin I leave my home
As now my love I say farewell.

The Fortinbras Proudfoot Esq. Foundation

In association with the Brisbane Tolkien Fellowship, Peter has formed the Fortinbras Proudfoot Esq. Foundation. The objective for the Foundation is that it be maintained as a non-profit organisation with a charter to raise funds for other charitable groups engaged in literacy initiatives and programs assisting children to enhance their education through literacy.

The main beneficiary of the group's fundraising is The Pyjama Foundation, whose volunteers assist the development of reading and writing skills of children in statutory and foster care.

The proceeds raised from this publication will go towards the purchase of books to support education programs assisting children in care.

More information about the foundation can be found at:
http://brisbanetolkienfellowship.com.au